For Jack! ♥ cg

BUDDY'S NEW BUDDY

ROBO CHARGERS

by **Christina Geist**
illustrated by **Tim Bowers**

Random House 🏠 New York

Text copyright © 2022 by Christina Geist
Jacket art and interior illustrations copyright © 2022 by Tim Bowers

All rights reserved. Published in the United States by Random House
Children's Books, a division of Penguin Random House LLC, New York.

Random House and the colophon are registered trademarks of Penguin Random House LLC.

Visit us on the Web! rhcbooks.com

Educators and librarians, for a variety of teaching tools, visit us at RHTeachersLibrarians.com

Library of Congress Cataloging-in-Publication Data is available upon request.
ISBN 978-0-593-30709-0 (trade) — ISBN 978-0-593-30710-6 (lib. bdg.) — ISBN 978-0-593-30711-3 (ebook)

The illustrations in this book were created digitally using Photoshop.
The text of this book is set in 18-point Cellini.
Interior design by Jan Gerardi

MANUFACTURED IN CHINA
10 9 8 7 6 5 4 3 2 1
First Edition

To my amazing nieces and nephews,
Drew & Kieran
Russell & Billy
Sloane, Elvis & Murphy
Frank, Bruce & Steve
—Your loving aunt Christi-nina, Crina, C.

To Caleb, Grady, and Brylie
—T.B.

Buddy wasn't feeling great.

His best buddy, who knew him better than anyone in the whole wide world, had just moved all the way across town.

"I know you're sad," said Mom. "But he's only a car ride away."

"We can make a playdate anytime!" said Dad.

Buddy knew they were right, but he was used to seeing his best buddy at school every day. They would high-five at their cubbies, play Robo Chargers at lunch, and practice karate at recess. Who was going to do all that stuff with him now? And a field trip to the natural history museum was coming up! They would be riding the bus with buddies, and Buddy didn't have a buddy anymore!

Thankfully, Lady had an idea. She was a really helpful big sister
who knew a lot about this stuff, and other stuff, too.

"How about making a new friend?" suggested Lady. "You just need to find something you have in common."

"In common?" asked Buddy.

"That means there is something about you that's the same. Something you both like to play or share or do together."

"Okay," said Buddy. "I'll try."

But the next day at school, Buddy didn't have
anything in common with anyone! No high fives.
No Robo Chargers. No karate. Nothing!
"It's okay," said Lady on the ride home.
"Tomorrow is a new day."

But tomorrow started out just like the day before. Until morning meeting, when Mr. Teacher said, "Class, this is Alison. She just moved here from all the way across town."

"Oh, my real, official name is Alison, but everyone just calls me Sunny," said the new girl.

Buddy could not believe his ears. He had a real, official name, too! And nobody called him that, either! Everybody just called him Buddy. He had never met anyone else with two names!

At lunch, Buddy decided to sit with Sunny, and he told her his real, official name. Nobody else at school knew it, so he whispered it and made her promise not to tell anyone. They sealed it with a secret friend handshake she'd learned from her big sister, who knew a lot about this kind of stuff, and other stuff, too.

The next day, Buddy could not believe his eyes. Sunny had Robo Chargers in her cubby! He'd never seen a girl with Robo Chargers. They high-fived until Mr. Teacher said, "Please be seated! Let's begin!"

At lunch, Sunny's Robo Chargers crushed Buddy's in a high-stakes battle for the galaxy. Then she taught him her secret strategy. She didn't mind sharing her secrets, or her cookies.

At recess, Buddy practiced his karate kicks while Sunny joined the dance group. Mr. Teacher noticed that karate and dance kicks had a lot in common!

The next day, Mr. Teacher said, "Don't forget our field trip! We'll be riding a bus to the natural history museum. I'll be pairing you with a buddy for the bus ride."

"Hey, Sunny, do you want to be my buddy?"

"Yes!"

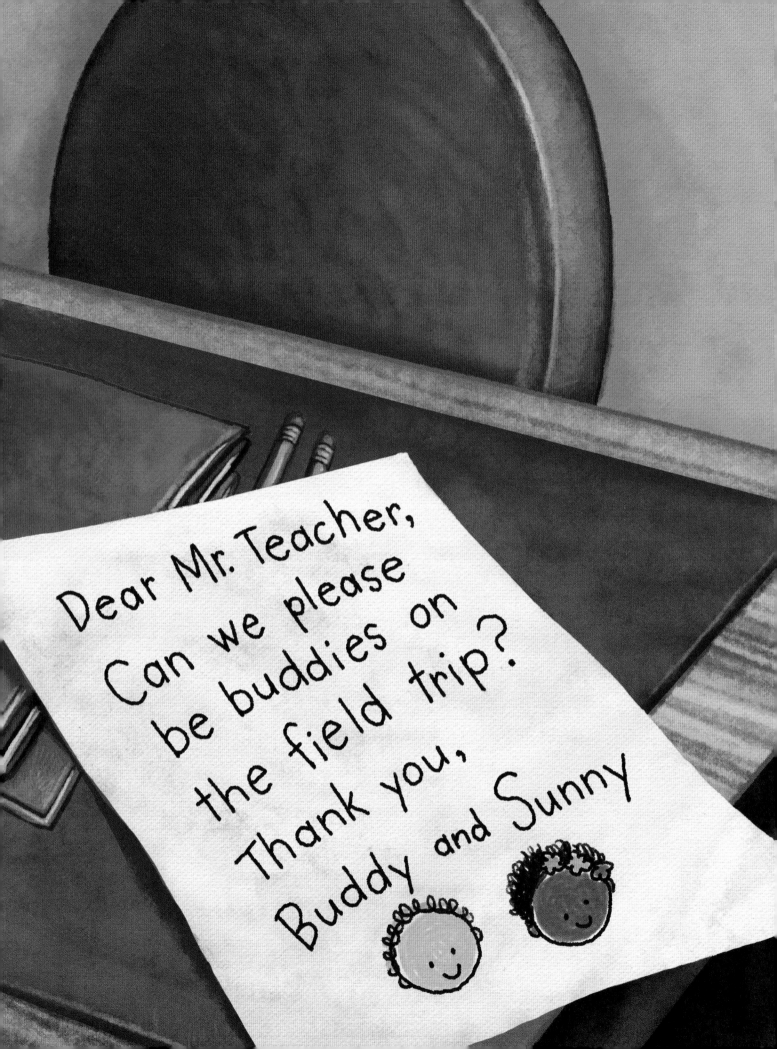

And the rest is history.

Voices
IN THE PARK

Anthony Browne

A DK INK BOOK
DK PUBLISHING, INC.

DK Publishing, Inc.
95 Madison Avenue
New York, New York 10016

Visit us on the World Wide Web at http://www.dk.com

Copyright © 1998 A.E.T Browne and Partners
Designed by Ian Butterworth

Printed and bound in Italy

First Edition, 1998
Published simultaneously in the United Kingdom
by Transworld Publishers Ltd.
2 4 6 8 10 9 7 5 3 1

Library of Congress Cataloging-in-Publication Data
Browne. Anthony.
Voices in the park/written and illustrated by Anthony Browne.–1st ed.
p. cm.
Summary: Lives briefly intertwine when two youngsters meet in the park.
ISBN 0-7894-2522-X
[1. Gorilla—Fiction. 2. Parks—Fiction. 3. Dogs—Fiction.]
I. Title.
PZ7.B81984Vo 1998
[E]--dc21   97-48730
CIP
AC

It was time to take Victoria, our pedigree Labrador, and Charles, our son, for a walk.

When we arrived at the park,
I let Victoria off her leash.
Immediately some scruffy
mongrel appeared and started
bothering her. I shooed it off,
but the horrible thing chased
her all over the park.

I ordered it to go away, but it took no notice of me whatsoever. "Sit," I said to Charles. "Here."

I was just planning what we should have to eat
that evening when I saw Charles had
disappeared. Oh dear! Where had he gone?

You get some frightful
types in the park these
days! I called his name for
what seemed like ages.

Then I saw him talking to
a very rough-looking child.
"Charles, come here. At
once!" I said. "And come
here please, Victoria."

We walked home in silence.

I needed to get out of the house, so me and Smudge took the dog to the park.

He loves it there. I wish I
had half the energy he's got.

I settled on a bench and looked through the paper for a job. I know it's a waste of time but you've got to have some hope, haven't you?

Then it was time to go. Smudge cheered me up. She chattered happily to me all the way home.

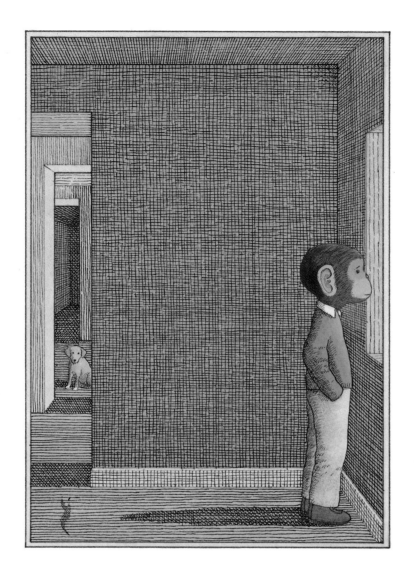

I was at home on my own again.
It's so boring. Then my mother
said that it was time for our walk.

There was a very friendly dog in the park, and
Victoria was having a great time. I wished I was.

"D'you wanna come on the slide?"
a voice asked. It was a girl,
unfortunately, but I went anyway.
She was great on the slide—she
went really fast. I was amazed.

The two dogs raced around like old friends.

The girl took off her
coat and swung on
the climbing bars, so I
did the same.

I'm good at climbing trees,
so I showed her how to do it.
She told me her name was
Smudge—a funny name, I know,
but she's nice. Then my mother
caught us talking together,
and I had to go home.

Maybe Smudge will be there next time?

Dad had been really fed up, so I was happy when he said we could take Albert to the park.

Albert's always in such a hurry to be let off
his leash. He went straight up to this nice dog
and sniffed its backside (he always does that).
Of course, the other dog didn't mind, but
its owner was really angry, the silly twit.

I got talking to this boy. I thought he was kind of a wimp at first, but he's okay. We played on the seesaw and he didn't say much, but later on he was more friendly.

We both burst out
laughing when we saw
Albert taking a swim.

Then we all played on
the bandstand, and I felt
really, really happy.

Charlie picked a flower
and gave it to me.

Then his mom called
him and he had to go.
He looked sad.

When I got home I put the flower in some
water, and made Dad a nice cup of cocoa.